W9-AVL-365

Lilly Traps the Bullies

Brenda Bellingham

Illustrated by Clarke MacDonald

Formac Publishing Company Limited

Halifax, Nova Scotia

Text copyright © 2011 by Brenda Bellingham
Illustrations copyright © 2011 by Clarke MacDonald
First published in the United States in 2012

All rights reserved. No part of this book may be reproduced or transmitted in
any form or by any means, electronic or mechanical, including photocopying,
or by any information storage or retrieval system, without permission in writing
from the publisher.

Formac Publishing Company Limited recognizes the support of the Province
of Nova Scotia through the Department of Tourism, Culture and Heritage.
We acknowledge the financial support of the Government of Canada through
the Canada Book Fund for our publishing activities. Formac Publishing
acknowledges the support of the Canada Council for the Arts which last year
invested $20.1 million in writing and publishing throughout Canada.

NOVA SCOTIA
Tourism, Culture and Heritage

The Canada Council | Le Conseil des Arts
for the Arts | du Canada

Canadä

Library and Archives Canada Cataloguing in Publication

Bellingham, Brenda, 1931-
     Lilly traps the bullies / Brenda Bellingham ; illustrations by
Clarke MacDonald.

(First novels)
Issued also in electronic format.
ISBN 978-0-88780-961-3 (bound). — ISBN 978-0-88780-959-0 (pbk.)
     I. MacDonald, Clarke (Clarke Robert). II. Title.
III. Series: First novels

PS8553.E468L544 2011   jC813'.54   C2011-903321-6

Formac Publishing Company Limited
5502 Atlantic Street
Halifax, Nova Scotia,
Canada B3H 1G4
www.formac.ca

Distributed in the United States by:
Orca Book Publishers
P.O. Box 468
Custer, WA USA
98240-0468

Printed and bound in Canada
Manufactured by Webcom in Toronto, Ontario, Canada in July, 2011.
Job # 378789

Love and thanks to my granddaughter, Katelyn,
and Timmy, the mouse, for their inspiration.

Table of Contents

1

What's Wrong?

There's no school tomorrow because of a teachers' convention. My parents have to go to work and my little brother will be at daycare. I'll be home alone.

"What can I do tomorrow?" I ask.

"Clean up your room," Mom says.

Boring!

Through our front window, I can see

Theresa and her mom. They live across the road.

Theresa's mom goes out to work. But her mom and dad are separated, so her dad doesn't live with them.

Theresa's face is red. She looks as though she's crying.

Her mom drives off, followed by a cloud of dust. The snow has gone but the salt and gravel haven't.

"I wonder what's wrong," I say. "I hope Boots is okay." Boots is Theresa's cat.

"Has Boots been sick lately?" Mom asks.

"No, but Theresa isn't a crybaby. She only cries about her cat."

"Maybe Theresa wanted to watch TV, but her mom made her go shopping," Mom says. "Theresa will tell you, or

not. You don't have to ask. Remember, curiosity killed the cat." This is one of my mom's favourite sayings.

"I can't help it if I'm curious. I care about my friends. We all care about each other."

Mom smiles. "I know. You have good friends, Lilly. You're lucky."

Mom's right. Minna, my best friend in the whole world, lives next door. Minna's parents own a store in Chinatown, but her grandma lives with them. When Minna's parents are away, her grandma takes care of Minna.

Minna, Theresa and I walk to and from school together. Sometimes Minna's grandma babysits Theresa. My parents are not home when I come home from school. I babysit myself, but if I have a problem I can go to Minna's grandma. It's good to have friends.

2

A Mouse in the House

"If you like you can go to the pool this afternoon," Mom says next morning. "Minna's grandma says she'll drive you."

There's public swimming because school is closed. They have extra lifeguards today, so we don't need an older girl to go with us.

"Is Theresa going?" I ask.

"Phone and ask her," Mom says. "But

don't bother Minna. She has to practice."

Minna wants to be a concert pianist when she grows up. She practices every day.

After my parents and my little brother leave, I phone Theresa. "Are you going to the pool this afternoon?"

"I can't," she says. "I have to find Timmy."

"Timmy?" I ask. "Who's Timmy?"

"A mouse," she says. "When I came home from school yesterday I opened the back door and there he was. He and Boots were staring at one another. Timmy was so scared he couldn't move, so I grabbed him."

"Wow," I say. "You were quick."

"I know. I was so scared Boots might

get him." She sighs. "But now I've lost him. Last night I made him a house. I put a bowl of water and a dish of food inside it. But he's gone. I can't find him anywhere."

"Don't worry. He'll turn up. Unless Boots caught him and ate him."

"He didn't. Boots slept on my bed all night. Timmy was in the basement."

"How do you know his name is Timmy?" I ask.

"I don't," she says. "That's what I call him. It suits him."

"So why can't you come to the pool?"

"We have to find Timmy. My mom says mice are dirty." Theresa's mom is a nurse. "Mom says they have diseases that humans can catch. She wants to set traps to kill him."

Now I know why Theresa was crying when I saw her. I don't have to ask.

3

A Humane Trap

"Buy a trap," I say, "one of those humane ones. You can set Timmy free after you catch him."

"Those traps cost a lot," Theresa says. "My mom says we can't afford one."

I suppose she's right. Theresa's mom is a single mom.

"Ordinary traps are humane too," I say.

"The mouse nibbles the cheese and —
BAM — it's dead. It doesn't suffer."

"It's still dead, isn't it? You're as bad as
Kendall's cousins."

I didn't know Kendall had any cousins.
"Are they nice?"

"No!" Theresa says. "They're boys.
One's called Spider and his little brother
is called Bugsy. They're mean. They were
at the store last night. They said we don't
need traps, and that I could cut off my
mouse's head with a carving knife."

"Like in the nursery rhyme, sort of." I
try not to giggle. "They were teasing you,
silly. Forget Timmy. Come to the pool
and have some fun."

"How can I enjoy myself when Timmy
might be lying dead at home?" She sniffs.

"But I want to go to the pool," I say. "Are you coming, or not?"

"NOT," Theresa says. "My mom's mad at me for bringing a mouse into the house. She thinks that Timmy might turn out to be Tammy. We could end up with a basement full of mice, but I don't want to kill Timmy. I want to make a humane trap. I want to catch Timmy without hurting him. Then I can take him somewhere outside and set him free. It's like they do with bears that hang around campgrounds. You don't have to murder a hungry animal. People are so cruel!" She's really sniffing now. I wish she'd blow her nose.

I feel sorry for being mean. "Listen," I say, "if you come to the pool with me,

I'll help you make a humane trap. We can find out how on the Web."

"You're sure?" she asks.

"Sure, I'm sure. You can find out how to do everything on the Web."

4

Theresa Needs Help

After lunch, Minna's grandma drives us to the pool. Theresa looks glum. She doesn't talk much. Kendall and his two cousins are already in the water. So is Heathrow. I like Heathrow, but Kendall — not so much. He thinks he knows everything.

Kendall's cousins don't seem to like him much either. Kendall is small for his

age and they call him "Kid." He looks a bit scared of them. They're nice to Heathrow though. And to me.

"Hi," I say. "I'm Lilly."

"Cute," the older one says.

I don't know if he means me, or my name. No one ever called me cute before. I try not to blush.

"I'm Spider," the bigger one says. "Call me Spy. This is Bugsy. Don't call him Bug."

"I wouldn't," I say. "No way."

Minna giggles.

Spider looks at her. "Are you the kid who plays the piano?"

Minna stops giggling. "Yes," she says.

"Why don't you and the other little kids go play together," Spider says. "Me and my brother are going on the big slide with Lill and Heathrow."

No one ever called me Lill before. It sounds much more grown-up than Lilly. I'm tall for my age, so maybe he thinks I'm older than I am. That's fine with me. The big slide hangs from the ceiling. It's fun.

Theresa glowers at me. I like that word — *glower*. Nobody can glower like Theresa. "I wish I'd stayed home," she says.

"Hey," Spider says. "Look! It's Mouse Woman. Caught your mouse yet?" Theresa doesn't answer.

"We'll do it for you," Bugsy says. "Chop, chop." He makes a chopping action with his hand.

"Anybody can go down the slide, Theresa," Heathrow says. "Go if you want to."

"But not with us," Spider says. "You kids go to the back of the line and stay out of our way."

5

At the Pool

"Bullies," Kendall mutters.

I think Bugsy is kind of cute. "Take no notice," I tell Kendall. "He was teasing."

"Only a lifeguard can stop kids using the slide," Minna says.

"Right," Kendall says. "Let's go."

I hurry to the slide. Minna, Theresa, and Kendall are slow. They come behind.

It's fun sliding down the long slide. Even climbing up the stairs to the top over and over again is fun. There's a lifeguard at the top to make sure we take turns. No pushing and shoving allowed!

Once, while I wait, I look down and see Theresa. She's on the deck, sitting on a chair, wrapped in her towel. I wonder if she's okay. The stairs are crowded, so I'll have to slide down before I can ask her.

Where are Minna and Kendall? It's hard to see my friends in the crowded pool. Heathrow waits in line ahead of me. Kendall's cousins are way behind. We're all separated by kids we don't know. It doesn't matter — everyone is friendly. Everyone is having fun. Everyone but Theresa.

At last it's my turn. As I climb out of the pool I see Minna. She pops her head out of the water and says something to Theresa. Theresa nods. Minna drops back into the pool. She and Kendall play ball. I should have known they wouldn't leave Theresa alone.

But Theresa looks upset, so I go to her. I bet she's still worried about that mouse.

"What's wrong?" I ask Theresa.

She glowers at me. "Spider tried to drown me."

"You're kidding."

"No, I'm not," she says. "He held on to my feet underwater. I couldn't breathe. Don't tell me he was only teasing. It wasn't funny."

I think that maybe she imagined it. "So

then what happened?"

"A lifeguard saw him and blew her whistle," Theresa says. "She made him get out of the pool. I couldn't hear what she said, but she looked mad."

"Time to go," Minna says. "Grandma will be waiting."

6

Lucky Me

After swimming, we wait in the lobby for Minna's grandma. "Hey, Lill, why don't you and Heath ride your bikes tomorrow?" Spy says. "You can grab a burger with me and Bugsy after swimming. Minna's grandma can drive the other kids."

Going for a burger sounds like fun — like we're teenagers. But I can't. "My bike's no good. I need a new tire." I hate to admit it.

"Borrow some wheels from a friend," Spy says. "What about your bike, Mouse Woman? Can Lill use it?"

Theresa turns away.

"Grandma can't drive us tomorrow," Minna says. "I have to practice for a piano competition."

Spy offers to shake her hand. "Best of luck," he says.

Minna quickly puts her hands behind her back. What's wrong with her?

"I might not be here either," Heathrow says. "I have to check at home first."

None of my friends seem to like Spy and Bugsy. "Why wouldn't you shake Bugsy's hand?" I ask Minna later.

"Because he'd squeeze it hard and hurt it," she says. "He's really mean."

I'm shocked. How does she know this about Spy?

When we get close to home, Theresa races ahead. We walk up the path just as she comes out of her house again. She looks disappointed. "My mouse house is empty," she says.

"Don't worry, Theresa," I say.

"You don't understand," Theresa says. "I have to make a humane trap. If I don't, my mom will set the killing kind." Her eyes fill with tears.

"So make a humane trap tomorrow," Minna says.

"I don't know how," Theresa says.

"Lilly will help you. Won't you, Lilly?" Minna says.

I don't want to make a humane trap. I'd rather go to the pool and hang out with Spy and Bugsy.

Sometimes I think that Minna can read my mind.

"Tell you what, Theresa," Minna says. "Tomorrow morning Lilly will help you make a humane trap. In return you can lend her your bike. Okay?"

"Okay," Theresa agrees. Lucky me!

7

Kendall Lends a Hand

The next morning I help Theresa with the trap. If we hurry I can go to the pool in the afternoon.

We look for "How to Make Humane Traps" on the Web. There's a list. We choose the easiest way. It says to use a plastic pop bottle. "We don't have any pop bottles," Theresa says. "I'm not allowed to drink pop. It makes you fat."

I'm skinny, but my mom says pop makes your teeth bad. Either way, we don't have any empty pop bottles. We can't phone Minna because she's practicing the piano. I phone Heathrow. His family doesn't drink pop. He doesn't say why. He says he'll phone Kendall. A few minutes later, Kendall arrives with some plastic water bottles. His mom drinks water at her keep fit class.

"Can I help?" Kendall says. "I don't want to go home. My cousins bug me."

"What about your little dog?" Theresa asks. "You can't leave him alone with them. Those bullies might tease him."

"He's okay," Kendall says. "When my cousins are around he goes to Heathrow's place. I know he's safe there. Heathrow's little sister really loves him."

It looks like I was wrong about Kendall. He is kinder than I thought.

"We need something to tempt Timmy to go in the bottle."

Theresa brings out some sunflower seeds. "I got them last Hallowe'en," she says. "But I don't like them. The husks are a nuisance. D'you think Timmy likes seeds?"

"Sure," I say. "He'll have to take the husks off first. That should keep him busy for a while."

Theresa drops the seeds into the bottle.

"How do we trap him inside?" she asks. "They sell fancy tops for the bottles on the Internet, I can't afford one of those."

"No problem," Kendall says. "Timmy's weight will tip the bottle and he'll slide down to the bottom where the seeds are."

"I have to go home for lunch now," Kendall says. "Then I have to go to the pool with my cousins."

"Me too," I say.

8

Lilly Has to Choose

"I'm not going to the pool," Theresa says. "I want to finish the humane trap for Timmy. You said you would help."

"I didn't know it would take so long," I say. "You promised to lend me your wheels this afternoon."

She glowers at me. "I keep my promises. You can take my bike. It's in the garage."

"Don't get mad," I say. "We don't really know how to make a humane trap, do we?"

"So we let Timmy die in one of those cruel wire traps." Her cheeks get red and her eyes fill with tears. It happens every time we talk about traps. I don't want to let Timmy die either. But I want to go to the pool. Most of all I want to go for a burger afterwards. It's the first time anyone ever asked me — apart from my parents. It makes me feel like a teenager.

Theresa turns her back on me. So what! Theresa isn't my best friend. Minna is. But...every day we three walk to school together. In summer we go to the playground together. I stand in the middle of the teeter-totter. I'm not supposed to, because it's dangerous. But I'm the biggest and strongest. Minna and Theresa sit one at each end. I bend my legs and make the teeter-totter ends go up and down. The other two squeal and laugh.

That gives me an idea. What if we tape a water bottle to a narrow piece of wood and prop the top up like a ramp? Timmy will run up the ramp until his weight tips the bottle. He'll slide down the ramp and into the seeds.

Minna shows up. Nobody had to ask her to come over. She comes because she thinks Theresa needs help. She's right. She pours some honey, not too much, into the bottom of the bottle. It's a tough job but Minna has clever fingers. I run home to get a roll of duct tape. You can make

anything work with duct tape. We tape the bottle to a narrow piece of wood. Then we prop it up like a ramp. It's fun when we work together. Theresa says the bottle with Timmy in it might fall and tip Timmy out. Just in case, we rig up a box to catch it. Theresa says Timmy can climb out of a cardboard box and escape. I find a plastic pail. Even a mouse can't climb a shiny plastic wall. The ramp can rest on top of the plastic pail too. We have to move the bottle so that its neck rests on the rim of the pail. More work with the duct tape. Bingo! Let him get out of that one.

When Theresa's mom comes home from work she's impressed with our trap.

"I'll give you one more night," she

9

Face Them Together

A mouse won't come out of hiding while anyone is around. We go outside. How long should we give Timmy to find the seeds? While we argue, Spy and Bugsy ride up on their bikes.

"Why didn't you and Heath come to the pool?" Spy asks me. "I thought we were going for burgers."

"I wonder what they'll do on Monday."

I don't want to think about it, but I do, all night. Early next morning the phone rings. My parents want to sleep in, so I answer it. It's Theresa.

"Timmy's in the trap," she says. "I'm going to take him to the park this afternoon. Do you want to come?"

Not really. "Are you scared?" I ask.

"Not for me," Theresa says. "But I'm scared for Timmy. What if those bullies hurt him? I couldn't bear that."

I remember how Theresa fought a neighbour once and saved a kitten. That's how she got her cat Boots. But can she fight Spider and Bugsy, two against one? I doubt it. She needs help.

"Listen," I say. "I'll go with you.

"I forgot," I say. It sounds like a pretty lame excuse.

"We were going to let you join our gang," he says. "Maybe we'll change our minds now."

Theresa makes things worse. "Lilly doesn't want to join your gang," she says. "Get lost, or I'll tell my mom you tried to drown me." She sounds very brave all of a sudden.

Spider and Bugsy laugh.

"Okay, Mouse Woman, see you at school on Monday," Bugsy says. "We'll get rid of your mouse for you." It sounds like a threat. They ride away.

I guess I was wrong about those two.

"We're lucky they think your mom is home," Minna says. She sounds gloomy.

Wrap Timmy's mouse house in some old birthday paper. I've got some. Make breathing holes. We'll pretend we're going to a party and the parcel is a gift. I'll carry it. We'll say it's a doll."

"You think that will work?" Theresa asks. "They might grab the parcel."

"Sure it will work. Mean guys don't play with dolls."

But what if Theresa is right? I have an idea. "You get a small cardboard box. Pretend Timmy is in it. That will fool them."

I sound a lot braver than I feel.

10

Free Timmy

I phone Minna and ask her to come with us to set Timmy free.

"Sure," she says. "I'll bring a wrapped gift too. We'll look as if we're all going to a party. Kendall should come too. They're *his* cousins."

"Not a good idea," Kendall says when I phone him to tell him our plan. "They'll beat me up. I'm smaller than they are."

"Minna is smaller than they are," I say. "So is Theresa. Ask Heathrow to come with you. He's not smaller."

"Heathrow isn't allowed to fight," Kendall says.

"Nobody is allowed to fight. We're not going to fight. We're going with Theresa, because we're her friends. Anyway, I have a plan."

Kendall sighs. "I hope it's a good one. Okay, I'll come."

As soon as we get to the park Spider and Bugsy show up. Surely they won't attack all five of us. But if they do, one of us can run for help.

"Look," I say. "Thanks for asking, but Heathrow and I don't want to join your gang."

"But you're both welcome to be friends with all of us," Heathrow says.

Spider and Bugsy laugh. "And play with dolls, like you guys?" Spider asks.

"Give us the mouse, Mouse Woman," Bugsy says.

"No way," Theresa says. She glowers at Bugsy and holds on to the box that doesn't have Timmy inside.

"I'll play with Lilly's dolly. It's bigger." Spy grabs my parcel.

I hold on as tightly as I can, but Spy is stronger. We struggle. The mouse house breaks. Out jumps Timmy — right to the ground. I'm scared he'll be killed, but he runs over Spider's feet.

Spider screams. "Help!" he yelps. "Get it away from me!"

"Yikes! A mouse!" Bugsy yells. "Don't let it get into the leg of your jeans." He and Spider jump on their bicycles and race away.

"Who'd think that those two bullies would be afraid of a little mouse?" Heathrow says.

"We should all get toy mice and keep them in our pockets," I say. "In case they try to bully us again."

"Don't worry," Kendall says. "my uncle has bought a house on the other side of town. Spider and Bugsy won't be going to our school."

Theresa crawls around in the long grass. "It's okay, Timmy," She calls out. "I only want to say goodbye. You don't have to be afraid. You're lucky. You have really good friends."

More novels in the
First Novels series!

Morgan and the Dune Racer

Ted Staunton

Illustrated by Bill Slavin

It's Morgan's birthday and all he wants is Charlie's remote-control toy — no matter what it takes or who he hurts to get it.

Mia, Matt and the

Mia, Matt and the Lazy Gator
Annie Langlois
Illustrated by Jimmy Beaulieu
Translated by Sarah Cummins

Mia and Matt can't wait to get to their uncle's summer cottage and find out what animal will be the star of their vacation. Will they be able to teach a lazy gator to dance?

Music by Morgan

Ted Staunton

Illustrated by Bill Slavin

Morgan has to get creative, and sneaky, if he wants to play music instead of floor hockey. He crafts a plan to swap places with Aldeen — but how long will they pull it off before they get caught?

Daredevil Morgan

Ted Staunton

Illustrated by Bill Slavin

Will Morgan be brave enough to try the GraviTwirl ride at the Fall Fair? Can he win the "Best Pumpkin Pie" contest, or will Aldeen Hummel, the Godzilla of Grade Three, interfere?

Raffi's For the Birds

Sylvain Meunier

Illustrated by Élisabeth Eudes-Pascal

Translated by Sarah Cummins

Raffi wants to save the birds by protesting the destruction of the trees they nest in. While he may have trouble walking, he has lots of ideas, and friends ready to help!